Songs for Little Folks

ILLUSTRATED BY

Terry Widener

STERLING

New York / London

Dedicated to Valentina, my granddaughter, who has reinvented fun,

taking life to a new level of wonderment and delight,

and, thankfully, bringing me along with her.

And in memoriam for Mary Travers, who made the delight of life become a powerful force. —P. Y.

To my children and my wife Leslie, and to my French agent, Michèle. —T. M. W.

STERLING and the distinctive Sterling logo are registered trademarks of Sterling Publishing Co., Inc.

Library of Congress Cataloging-in-Publication Data

The Peter Yarrow songbook : Songs for Little Folks / illustrated by Terry Widener.   v. cm.

Contents: Polly wolly doodle -- Pop! Goes the weasel -- Old MacDonald had a farm -- Oh dear, what can the matter be? --

This old man -- Billy Boy -- The green grass grew -- Mary had a little lamb --

Ten little puppy dogs -- A-tisket, a-tasket -- Lavender blue -- Row, row, row your boat.

ISBN 978-1-4027-5964-2

1. Children's songs, English--Texts. [1. Songs.] I. Yarrow, Peter, 1938- II. Widener, Terry, ill. III. Title: Songs for Little Folk.

PZ8.3.P4426 2010

782.42083--dc22

2009018957

Lot #:

2   4   6   8   10   9   7   5   3   1

02/10

Published by Sterling Publishing Co., Inc.

387 Park Avenue South, New York, NY 10016

All songs are traditional with new lyrics and music by Peter Yarrow and Bethany Yarrow © 2010

Silver Dawn Music, ASCAP

Additional text © 2010 by Peter Yarrow

Illustrations © 2010 by Terry Widener

Distributed in Canada by Sterling Publishing

c/o Canadian Manda Group, 165 Dufferin Street

Toronto, Ontario, Canada M6K 3H6

Distributed in the United Kingdom by GMC Distribution Services Castle Place,

166 High Street, Lewes, East Sussex, England BN7 1XU

Distributed in Australia by Capricorn Link (Australia) Pty. Ltd.

P.O. Box 704, Windsor, NSW 2756, Australia

Sterling ISBN 978-1-4027-5964-2

For information about custom editions, special sales, premium and corporate purchases, please contact

Sterling Special Sales Department at 800-805-5489 or specialsales@sterlingpublishing.com.

The artwork for this book was created using acrylic paints.

CONTENTS

PETER YARROW

In this, my fourth book in a series of which I am greatly proud, my daughter Bethany and I have recorded 12 songs for little ones who are about the age of Bethany's daughter, Valentina, now two and a half. Valentina simply adores these books. Sometimes, I sit down and page through them and sing the songs to her, and sometimes I just play the CD and point to the words and the images when they relate. These are some of the sweetest, most intimate and happy times that Valentina and I share. Yes, she knows it's her "Appa" singing on the CD with her "Mama," but I think that her love of these books stands by itself, too.

One evening, while sharing these songs with Valentina before bedtime, I had an ironic thought. With a sigh, somewhat wistfully, I said to Bethany, "I wish these books had existed when you were Valentina's age." She knew what I meant and smiled a mother's smile and a daughter's smile, both at the same time. I didn't realize until later what a compliment the grandfather in me had given the folk singer in me, as well as the magical, inspiring folk music that has now been handed down to Valentina, who one day might sing these same songs to her daughter. What a lovely thought!

The Green Grass Grew

There was a hole in the middle of the ground,
The prettiest little hole that you ever did see.
Well, the hole in the ground,
And the green grass grew all around, all around,
And the green grass grew all around.

And in this hole there was a tree,
The prettiest little tree that you ever did see.
Well, the tree in the hole,
And the hole in the ground,
And the green grass grew all around, all around,
And the green grass grew all around.

And on this tree there was a branch,
The prettiest little branch that you ever did see.
Well, the branch on the tree,
And the tree in the hole,
And the hole in the ground,
And the green grass grew all around, all around,
And the green grass grew all around.

And on this branch there was a nest,
The prettiest little nest that you ever did see.
Well, the nest on the branch,
And the branch on the tree,
And the tree in the hole,
And the hole in the ground,
And the green grass grew all around, all around,
And the green grass grew all around.

And in this nest there was an egg,
The prettiest little egg that you ever did see.
Well, the egg in the nest,
And the nest on the branch,
And the branch on the tree,
And the tree in the hole,
And the hole in the ground,
And the green grass grew all around, all around,
And the green grass grew all around.

And on this egg there was a bird,
The prettiest little bird that you ever did see.
Well, the bird on the egg,
And the egg in the nest,
And the nest on the branch,
And the branch on the tree,
And the tree in the hole,
And the hole in the ground,
And the green grass grew all around, all around,
And the green grass grew all around.

And on this bird there was a feather,
The prettiest little feather that you ever did see.
Well, the feather on the bird,
And the bird on the egg,
And the egg in the nest,
And the nest on the branch,
And the branch on the tree,
And the tree in the hole,
And the hole in the ground,
And the green grass grew all around, all around,
And the green grass grew all around.

8

A-Tisket, A-Tasket

A-tisket, a-tasket,
A green and yellow basket.
I wrote a letter to my love
And on the way I dropped it.

I dropped it, I dropped it,
Yes, on the way I dropped it.
A little girl, she picked it up
And took it to the market.

It was for him and no one else,
So no one else can read it.
I told him that I loved him so,
I hope that no one sees it.

A-tisket, a-tasket,
A green and yellow basket.
I wrote a letter to my love
And on the way I dropped it.

I dropped it, I dropped it,
On the way I dropped it.
A little girl she picked it up
And took it to the market.

Pop! Goes the Weasel

All around the mulberry bush
The monkey chased the weasel.
The monkey thought it was all in fun.
Pop! goes the weasel.

I've no time to waste my time,
I've no time to wheedle.
Kiss me quick and then I'm gone.
Pop! goes the weasel.

10

A penny for a spool of thread,
A penny for a needle.
That's the way the money goes.
Pop! goes the weasel.

I've no time to waste my time,
I've no time to wheedle.
Kiss me quick and then I'm gone.
Pop! goes the weasel.

Half a pound of tuppenny rice,
Half a pound of treacle.
Mix it up and make it nice.
Pop! goes the weasel.

I've no time to waste my time,
I've no time to wheedle.
Kiss me quick and then I'm gone.
Pop! goes the weasel.

Mary Had A Little Lamb

Mary had a little lamb,
Little lamb, little lamb.
Mary had a little lamb
Whose fleece was white as snow.

And everywhere that Mary went,
Mary went, Mary went,
Everywhere that Mary went, the lamb was sure to go.

It followed her to school one day,
School one day, school one day.
It followed her to school one day, which was
    against the rules.
It made the children laugh and play,
Laugh and play, laugh and play.
It made the children laugh and play to see
    a lamb at school.

But then the teacher turned it out,
Turned it out, turned it out.
But then the teacher turned it out, but still it lingered near,
And waited patiently about,
-ly about, -ly about,
And waited patiently about till Mary did appear.

"Why does the lamb love Mary so,
Mary so, Mary so?
Why does the lamb love Mary so?" the eager children cry.
"'Cause Mary loves the lamb, you know,
Lamb, you know, lamb, you know.
'Cause Mary loves the lamb, you know," the teacher did reply.

Mary had a little lamb,
Little lamb, little lamb.
Mary had a little lamb
Whose fleece was white as snow.

Row, Row, Row Your Boat

Row, row, row your boat,
Gently down the stream.
Merrily, merrily, merrily, merrily,
Life is but a dream.

Lavender Blue

Lavender blue, dilly, dilly, rosemary green,
When I am king, dilly, dilly, you shall be queen.
Who told you so, dilly, dilly, who told you so?
'Twas my own heart, dilly, dilly, that much I know.

Lavender blue, dilly, dilly, rosemary green,
If you love me, dilly, dilly, it shall be seen.
Let the birds sing, dilly, dilly, let the lambs play,
We shall be safe, dilly, dilly, out of harm's way.

Lavender blue, dilly, dilly, rosemary green,
When I am king, dilly, dilly, you shall be queen.
Who told you so, dilly, dilly, who told you so?
'Twas my own heart, dilly, dilly, that much I know.

Oh Dear, What Can the Matter Be?

Oh dear, what can the matter be?
Dear, dear, what can the matter be?
Oh dear, what can the matter be?
Johnny's so long at the fair.

He promised he'd buy me a fairing should please me,
And then, for a kiss, he vowed he would tease me.
He promised to bring me a bunch of blue ribbons
To tie up my bonny brown hair.

Oh dear, what can the matter be?
Dear, dear, what can the matter be?
Oh dear, what can the matter be?
Johnny's so long at the fair.

He promised to buy me a pair of sleeve buttons,
A pair of new garters that cost him but tuppence.
He promised he'd bring me a bunch of blue ribbons
To tie up my bonny brown hair.

Oh dear, what can the matter be?
Dear, dear, what can the matter be?
Oh dear, what can the matter be?
Johnny's so long at the fair.

He promised he'd bring me a basket of posies,
A garland of lilies, a garland of roses,
A little straw hat to set off the blue ribbons
To tie up my bonny brown hair.

Oh dear, what can the matter be?
Dear, dear, what can the matter be?
Oh dear, what can the matter be?
Johnny's so long at the fair.

Billy Boy

Oh, where have you been,
Billy Boy, Billy Boy?
Oh, where have you been, charming Billy?
I have been to see my wife.
She's the darling of my life.
She's a young thing and she cannot leave her mother.

Did she ask you to come in,
Billy Boy, Billy Boy?
Did she ask you to come in, charming Billy?
Yes, she asked me to come in,
With a dimple on her chin.
She's a young thing and she cannot leave her mother.

Did she set for you a chair,
Billy Boy, Billy Boy?
Did she set for you a chair, charming Billy?
Yes, she set for me a chair,
With her ringlets in her hair.
She's a young thing and she cannot leave her mother.

But can she bake a cherry pie,
Billy Boy, Billy boy?
Can she bake a cherry pie, charming Billy?
Yes, she can bake a cherry pie,
Quick as a cat can wink its eye.
She's a young thing and she cannot leave her mother.

Oh, where have you been,
Billy Boy, Billy Boy?
Oh, where have you been, charming Billy?
I have been to see my wife.
She's the darling of my life.
She's a young thing and she cannot leave her mother.

21

Ten little, nine little, eight little kitty cats,
Seven little, six little, five little kitty cats,
Four little, three little, two little kitty cats,
One little kitty cat now.

Ten Little Puppy Dogs

One little, two little, three little puppy dogs,
Four little, five little, six little puppy dogs,
Seven little, eight little, nine little puppy dogs,
Ten little puppy dogs now.

Ten little, nine little, eight little puppy dogs,
Seven little, six little, five little puppy dogs,
Four little, three little, two little puppy dogs,
One little puppy dog now.

One little, two little, three little kitty cats,
Four little, five little, six little kitty cats,
Seven little, eight little, nine little kitty cats,
Ten little kitty cats now.

One little, two little, three little chickadees,
Four little, five little, six little chickadees,
Seven little, eight little, nine little chickadees,
Ten little chickadees now.

Ten little, nine little, eight little chickadees,
Seven little, six little, five little chickadees,
Four little, three little, two little chickadees,
One little chickadee now.

One little, two little, three little porcupines,
Four little, five little, six little porcupines,
Seven little, eight little, nine little porcupines,
Ten little porcupines now.

Ten little, nine little, eight little porcupines,
Seven little, six little, five little porcupines,
Four little, three little, two little porcupines,
One little porcupine now.

This Old Man

This old man, he played one,
He played knick-knack on my thumb.
With a knick-knack, paddy-whack,
Give your dog a bone,
This old man came rolling home.

This old man, he played two,
He played knick-knack on my shoe.
With a knick-knack, paddy-whack,
Give your dog a bone,
This old man came rolling home.

This old man, he played three,
He played knick-knack on my knee.
With a knick-knack, paddy-whack,
Give your dog a bone,
This old man came rolling home.

This old man, he played four,
He played knick-knack at my door.
With a knick-knack, paddy-whack,
Give your dog a bone,
This old man came rolling home.

This old man, he played five,
He played folk and jazz and jive.
With a knick-knack, paddy-whack,
Give your dog a bone,
This old man came rolling home.

This old man, he played six,
He played knick-knack with his sticks.
With a knick-knack, paddy-whack,
Give your dog a bone,
This old man came rolling home.

Polly Wolly Doodle

Oh, I went down south to see my gal,
Singing Polly wolly doodle all the day.
O, my Sal, she is a spunky gal,
Singing Polly wolly doodle all the day.

Fare thee well, fare thee well,
Fare thee well, my fair young maid,
'Cause I'm going to Lou'siana
For to see my Susyanna,
Singing Polly wolly doodle all the day.

Oh, my Sal, she is a lady fair,
Singing Polly wolly doodle all the day,
With laughing eyes and curly hair,
Singing Polly wolly doodle all the day.

Fare thee well, fare thee well,
Fare thee well, my fair young maid,
'Cause I'm going to Lou'siana
For to see my Susyanna,
Singing Polly wolly doodle all the day.

My Sal, she can dance the whole night long,
Polly wolly doodle all the day,
Just as long as I'm singin' her this song,
Polly wolly doodle all the day.

Fare thee well, fare thee well,
Fare thee well, my fair young maid,
'Cause I'm going to Lou'siana
For to see my Susyanna,
Singing Polly wolly doodle all the day.

Oh, a grasshopper's sittin' on a railroad track,
Polly wolly doodle all the day,
A-pickin' his teeth with a carpet tack,
Polly wolly doodle all the day.

Fare thee well, fare thee well,
Fare thee well, my fair young maid,
'Cause I'm going to Lou'siana
For to see my Susyanna,
Singing Polly wolly doodle all the day.

Old MacDonald Had a Farm

Old MacDonald had a farm, E-I-E-I-O.
And on that farm there was a cow, E-I-E-I-O.
With a "moo-moo" here, and a "moo-moo" there,
Here a "moo," there a "moo,"
Everywhere a "moo-moo."

Old MacDonald had a farm, E-I-E-I-O.
And on that farm there was a pig, E-I-E-I-O.
With an "oink-oink" here, and an "oink-oink" there,
Here an "oink," there an "oink,"
Everywhere an "oink-oink."

Old MacDonald had a farm, E-I-E-I-O.
And on that farm he had a chicken, E-I-E-I-O.
With a "bawk-bawk" here, and a "bawk-bawk" there,
Here a "bawk," there a "bawk,"
Everywhere a "bawk-bawk."

Old MacDonald had a farm, E-I-E-I-O.
And on that farm he had a goat, E-I-E-I-O.
With a "nee" here, and a "nee" there,
Here a "nee," there a "nee,"
Everywhere a "nee-nee."

Old MacDonald had a farm, E-I-E-I-O.
And on that farm there was a sheep, E-I-E-I-O.
With a "baa-baa" here, and a "baa-baa" there,
Here a "baa," there a "baa,"
Everywhere a "baa-baa."

Old MacDonald had a farm, E-I-E-I-O.
And on that farm there were some ants, E-I-E-I-O.
With a "chk-a-chk-a" here, and a "chk-a-chk-a" there,
Here a "chk-a-chk-a," there a "chk-a-chk-a,"
Everywhere a "chk-a-chk-a."

Old MacDonald had a farm, E-I-E-I-O.
And on that farm there were some dogs, E-I-E-I-O.
With a "woof-woof" here, and a "woof-woof" there,
Here a "woof," there a "woof,"
Everywhere a "woof-woof."
Old MacDonald had a farm, E-I-E-I-O.

29

NOTES TO MY FELLOW "PICKERS"

As you review the lyrics to the songs printed on the following pages, you will see the chord names (with diagrams showing you where to put your fingers on the strings) above the words indicating where each new chord begins.

Please don't feel you have to stick with the chords I'm playing at all. I'm always changing and developing my accompaniments—sometimes I change back to earlier chord patterns, then return again. In folk music, making these changes is not only allowed, it's expected and admired as part of a music that celebrates the gifts of each individual to interpret the music as he or she sees fit. Making changes to a folk song is called "the folk process," which means that new players change the song's lyrics, melody, rhythmic feel, and accompaniment to suit themselves and make the songs feel right and relevant in their own times.

Have fun creating your own folk process.
The songs will appreciate it and feel loved, I promise you.

The Green Grass Grew

D

There was a hole in the middle of the ground,

A

The prettiest little hole that you ever did see.

D

Well, the hole in the ground,

A   D   G

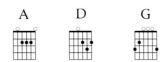

And the green grass grew all a-round, all a-round,

D   A   D

And the green grass grew all a-round.

And in this hole there was a tree,
The prettiest little tree that you ever did see.
Well, the tree in the hole,
And the hole in the ground,
And the green grass grew all around, all around,
And the green grass grew all around.

And on this tree there was a branch,
The prettiest little branch that you ever did see.
Well, the branch on the tree,
And the tree in the hole,
And the hole in the ground,
And the green grass grew all around, all around,
And the green grass grew all around.

And on this branch there was a nest,
The prettiest little nest that you ever did see.
Well, the nest on the branch,
And the branch on the tree,
And the tree in the hole,
And the hole in the ground,
And the green grass grew all around, all around,
And the green grass grew all around.

And in this nest there was an egg,
The prettiest little egg that you ever did see.
Well, the egg in the nest,
And the nest on the branch,
And the branch on the tree,
And the tree in the hole,
And the hole in the ground,
And the green grass grew all around, all around,
And the green grass grew all around.

And on this egg there was a bird,
The prettiest little bird that you ever did see.
Well, the bird on the egg,
And the egg in the nest,
And the nest on the branch,
And the branch on the tree,
And the tree in the hole,
And the hole in the ground,
And the green grass grew all around, all around,
And the green grass grew all around.

And on this bird there was a feather,
The prettiest little feather that you ever did see.
Well, the feather on the bird,
And the bird on the egg,
And the egg in the nest,
And the nest on the branch,
And the branch on the tree,
And the tree in the hole,
And the hole in the ground,
And the green grass grew all around, all around,
And the green grass grew all around.

A-Tisket, A-Tasket

D

A-tisket, a-tasket,

D

A green and yellow basket.

A

I wrote a letter to my love

D

And on the way I dropped it.

D

I dropped it, I dropped it,

D

Yes, on the way I dropped it.

A

A little girl, she picked it up

D

And took it to the market.

G   **F♯m**

It was for him and no one else,

Em   **D**

So no one else can read it.

G   **F♯m**

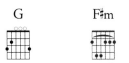

I told him that I loved him so,

Em   **A**

I hope that no one sees it.

A-tisket, a-tasket,
A green and yellow basket.
I wrote a letter to my love
And on the way I dropped it.

I dropped it, I dropped it,
On the way I dropped it.
A little girl she picked it up
And took it to the market.

Pop! Goes the Weasel

C G C

All a-round the mulberry bush

C G C

The monkey chased the weasel.

C G C

The monkey thought it was all in fun.

F G C

Pop! goes the weasel.

Am Em

I've no time to waste my time,

Am Em

I've no time to wheedle.

Dm7

Kiss me quick and then I'm gone.

F G C

Pop! goes the weasel.

A penny for a spool of thread,
A penny for a needle.
That's the way the money goes.
Pop! goes the weasel.

I've no time to waste my time,
I've no time to wheedle.
Kiss me quick and then I'm gone.
Pop! goes the weasel.

Half a pound of tuppenny rice,
Half a pound of treacle.
Mix it up and make it nice.
Pop! goes the weasel.

I've no time to waste my time,
I've no time to wheedle.
Kiss me quick and then I'm gone.
Pop! goes the weasel.

Mary Had a Little Lamb

E

Mary had a little lamb,

B7   E

Little lamb, little lamb.

E

Mary had a little lamb

B7   E

Whose fleece was white as snow.

E

And everywhere that Mary went,

B7   E

Mary went, Mary went,

E   B7   E

Everywhere that Mary went, the lamb was sure to go.

It followed her to school one day,
School one day, school one day.
It followed her to school one day, which was against the rules.
It made the children laugh and play,
Laugh and play, laugh and play.
It made the children laugh and play to see a lamb at school.

But then the teacher turned it out,
Turned it out, turned it out.
But then the teacher turned it out, but still it lingered near,
And waited patiently about,
-ly about, -ly about,
And waited patiently about till Mary did appear.

"Why does the lamb love Mary so,
Mary so, Mary so?
Why does the lamb love Mary so?" the eager children cry.
"'Cause Mary loves the lamb, you know,
Lamb, you know, lamb, you know.
'Cause Mary loves the lamb, you know," the teacher did reply.

Mary had a little lamb,
Little lamb, little lamb.
Mary had a little lamb
Whose fleece was white as snow.

Row, Row, Row Your Boat

D

Row, row, row your boat,

D

Gently down the stream.

D

Merrily, merrily, merrily, merrily,

D

Life is but a dream.

Lavender Blue

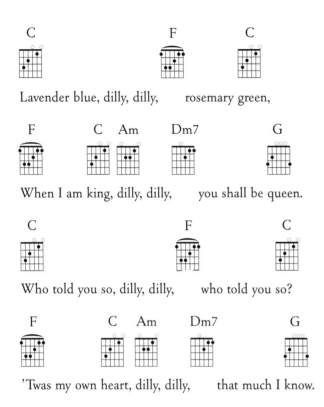

Lavender blue, dilly, dilly,   rosemary green,

When I am king, dilly, dilly,   you shall be queen.

Who told you so, dilly, dilly,   who told you so?

'Twas my own heart, dilly, dilly,   that much I know.

Lavender blue, dilly, dilly, rosemary green,
If you love me, dilly, dilly, it shall be seen.
Let the birds sing, dilly, dilly, let the lambs play,
We shall be safe, dilly, dilly, out of harm's way.

Lavender blue, dilly, dilly, rosemary green,
When I am king, dilly, dilly, you shall be queen.
Who told you so, dilly, dilly, who told you so?
'Twas my own heart, dilly, dilly, that much I know.

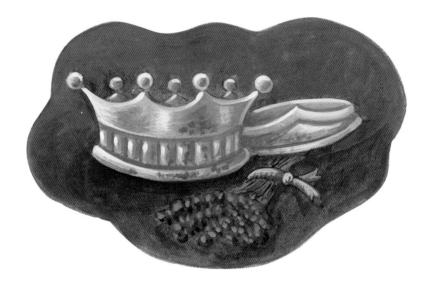

Oh Dear, What Can the Matter Be?

C

Oh dear, what can the matter be?

Dm   G

Dear, dear, what can the matter be?

C

Oh dear, what can the matter be?

Dm   G   C

Johnny's so long at the fair.

C

He promised he'd buy me a fairing should please me,

Dm   G

And then, for a kiss, he vowed he would tease me.

C

He promised to bring me a bunch of blue ribbons

Dm   G   C

To tie up my bonny brown hair.

Oh dear, what can the matter be?
Dear, dear, what can the matter be?
Oh dear, what can the matter be?
Johnny's so long at the fair.

He promised to buy me a pair of sleeve buttons,
A pair of new garters that cost him but tuppence.
He promised he'd bring me a bunch of blue ribbons
To tie up my bonny brown hair.

Oh dear, what can the matter be?
Dear, dear, what can the matter be?
Oh dear, what can the matter be?
Johnny's so long at the fair.

He promised he'd bring me a basket of posies,
A garland of lilies, a garland of roses,
A little straw hat to set off the blue ribbons
To tie up my bonny brown hair.

Oh dear, what can the matter be?
Dear, dear, what can the matter be?
Oh dear, what can the matter be?
Johnny's so long at the fair.

Billy Boy

C

Oh, where have you been,

C

Billy Boy, Billy Boy?

G

Oh, where have you been, charming Billy?

G

I have been to see my wife.

C   Em

She's the darling of my life.

F   C   G   C
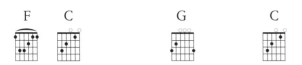

She's a young thing and she cannot leave her mother.

Did she ask you to come in,
Billy Boy, Billy Boy?
Did she ask you to come in, charming Billy?
Yes, she asked me to come in,
With a dimple on her chin.
She's a young thing and she cannot leave her mother.

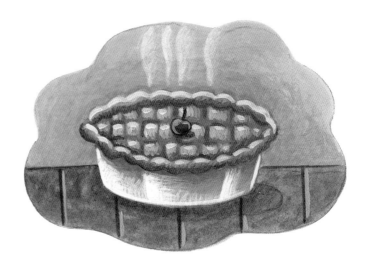

Did she set for you a chair,
Billy Boy, Billy Boy?
Did she set for you a chair, charming Billy?
Yes, she set for me a chair,
With her ringlets in her hair.
She's a young thing and she cannot leave her mother.

But can she bake a cherry pie,
Billy Boy, Billy boy?
Can she bake a cherry pie, charming Billy?
Yes, she can bake a cherry pie,
Quick as a cat can wink its eye.
She's a young thing and she cannot leave her mother.

Oh, where have you been,
Billy Boy, Billy Boy?
Oh, where have you been, charming Billy?
I have been to see my wife.
She's the darling of my life.
She's a young thing and she cannot leave her mother.

Ten Little Puppy Dogs

C

One little, two little, three little puppy dogs,

G

Four little, five little, six little puppy dogs,

C

Seven little, eight little, nine little puppy dogs,

G   C

Ten little puppy dogs now.

Ten little, nine little, eight little puppy dogs,
Seven little, six little, five little puppy dogs,
Four little, three little, two little puppy dogs,
One little puppy dog now.

One little, two little, three little kitty cats,
Four little, five little, six little kitty cats,
Seven little, eight little, nine little kitty cats,
Ten little kitty cats now.

Ten little, nine little, eight little kitty cats,
Seven little, six little, five little kitty cats,
Four little, three little, two little kitty cats,
One little kitty cat now.

One little, two little, three little chickadees,
Four little, five little, six little chickadees,
Seven little, eight little, nine little chickadees,
Ten little chickadees now.

Ten little, nine little, eight little chickadees,
Seven little, six little, five little chickadees,
Four little, three little, two little chickadees,
One little chickadee now.

One little, two little, three little porcupines,
Four little, five little, six little porcupines,
Seven little, eight little, nine little porcupines,
Ten little porcupines now.

Ten little, nine little, eight little porcupines,
Seven little, six little, five little porcupines,
Four little, three little, two little porcupines,
One little porcupine now.

This Old Man

C

This old man, he played one,

F   G

He played knick-knack on my thumb.

C

With a knick-knack, paddy-whack,

C

Give your dog a bone,

G   C

This old man came rolling home.

This old man, he played two,
He played knick-knack on my shoe.
With a knick-knack, paddy-whack,
Give your dog a bone,
This old man came rolling home.

This old man, he played three,
He played knick-knack on my knee.
With a knick-knack, paddy-whack,
Give your dog a bone,
This old man came rolling home.

This old man, he played four,
He played knick-knack at my door.
With a knick-knack, paddy-whack,
Give your dog a bone,
This old man came rolling home.

This old man, he played five,
He played folk and jazz and jive.
With a knick-knack, paddy-whack,
Give your dog a bone,
This old man came rolling home.

This old man, he played six,
He played knick-knack with his sticks.
With a knick-knack, paddy-whack,
Give your dog a bone,
This old man came rolling home.

Polly Wolly Doodle

E

Oh, I went down south to see my gal,

B7

Singing Polly wolly doodle all the day.

B7

O, my Sal, she is a spunky gal,

E

Singing Polly wolly doodle all the day.

E

Fare thee well, fare thee well,

B7

Fare thee well, my fair young maid,

B7

'Cause I'm going to Lou'siana

B7

For to see my Susyanna,

E

Singing Polly wolly doodle all the day.

Oh, my Sal, she is a lady fair,
Singing Polly wolly doodle all the day,
With laughing eyes and curly hair,
Polly wolly doodle all the day.

Fare thee well, fare thee well,
Fare thee well, my fair young maid,
'Cause I'm going to Lou'siana
For to see my Susyanna,
Singing Polly wolly doodle all the day.

My Sal, she can dance the whole night long,
Polly wolly doodle all the day,
Just as long as I'm singin' her this song,
Polly wolly doodle all the day.

Fare thee well, fare thee well,
Fare thee well, my fair young maid,
'Cause I'm going to Lou'siana
For to see my Susyanna,
Singing Polly wolly doodle all the day.

Oh, a grasshopper's sittin' on a railroad track,
Polly wolly doodle all the day,
A-pickin' his teeth with a carpet tack,
Polly wolly doodle all the day.

Fare thee well, fare thee well,
Fare thee well, my fair young maid,
'Cause I'm going to Lou'siana
For to see my Susyanna,
Singing Polly wolly doodle all the day.

Old MacDonald Had a Farm

G   C   G   D   G

Old MacDonald had a farm, E - I - E - I - O.

          C   G   D   G

And on that farm there was a cow, E - I - E - I - O.

          G

With a "moo-moo" here, and
   a "moo-moo" there,
Here a "moo," there a "moo,"
Everywhere a "moo-moo."

G   C   G   D   G

Old MacDonald had a farm, E - I - E - I - O.

Em   B7 Em   B7 Em

Old MacDonald had a farm, E - I - E - I - O.

          B7   Em   B7 Em

And on that farm there were some ants, E - I - E - I - O.

          Em

With a "chk-a-chk-a" here, and
   a "chk-a-chk-a" there,
Here a "chk-a-chk-a," there a "chk-a-chk-a,"
Everywhere a "chk-a-chk-a."

G   C   G   D   G

Old MacDonald had a farm, E - I - E - I - O.

(Please see page 28 for additional lyrics.)

About the Songs

The Green Grass Grew

This American folk song was written about 100 years ago by William Jerome and Harry Von Tilzer. When we sing it together, it can be a fun game to see who can remember which words come next as the verses grow longer and longer. A picture of a hole in the ground, a tree in the hole, a branch on the tree, a bird on the branch—and on and on—is created in our minds, and that's part of the fun. Folk songs like this use what is called "incremental repetition," which is a fancy way to say that each time we repeat a verse we add a little bit more (an increment) to the lyrics. Can you make up even more verses to this song?

A-Tisket, A-Tasket

This song was created over a hundred years ago but, like many folk songs, no one knows exactly who wrote it. With folk songs, it's expected that over the years people will change the words and music to suit themselves. This is known as the "folk process." In this book's version of "A-Tisket, A-Tasket," as my contribution to the folk process, I added words and music to make a new chorus because, when I sing it, I want to share the idea that the girl in the song has only just admitted to herself that she's fallen in love. She has not yet told anyone, and she wants her love to be a secret until, and if, she herself tells the man she loves.

Pop! Goes the Weasel

A sheet of music from 1853 at the British Library mentions "Pop Goes the Weasel," which was written much earlier. To me, the song's special, hidden message is that we have many moments of our lives, which, like pennies, get spent a little here and a little there. If we think of these small moments as pennies, we can see that tiny problems quickly come and go. Rather than focusing on small "pennies," we should try to see the real wealth of life and be grateful for those things that truly matter, like family, friends, and the beauty of a song or a flower. Of course there's love, too, which is perhaps most important of all.

Mary Had a Little Lamb

This song was written about an event that happened to a young girl almost 200 years ago in the town of Sterling, Massachusetts. Mary Sawyer took her pet lamb to school one day and it caused a great commotion. John Roulstone, a young man who was visiting the school, described it in a poem and gave it to Sarah Josepha Hale, who added more verses and published it in 1830 as a nursery rhyme. Later, Lowell Mason wrote a melody and the song became famous. A statue of Mary's little lamb still stands in the Sterling town center.

Row, Row, Row Your Boat

This song is over 150 years old and is one of my favorite rounds. A round is a song where two or more people sing the same melody, but the singers start at different times. Try it, and after a while, singing rounds will get a lot easier. To me, my favorite line, "Life is but a dream," gives us a hint about how to live a happy and meaningful life. I believe that feelings are like dreams in many ways. Acknowledging our feelings can determine how happy or unhappy we are. If we are able to reach for our most loving, caring, and grateful feelings, our lives will flow "gently down the stream" and we will appreciate the beautiful things the world has to offer— and leave most of our troubles behind.

Lavender Blue

This song from England is more than 300 years old. Spices like parsley, sage, and rosemary, and flowers like lavender and posies, are very popular in love songs from long ago. This song was written in a time of kings and queens, knights and peasants, lords and ladies. So when I sing it, I imagine that I am a farm boy, without much at all in the world. I imagine that I'm taking a break from working and all of a sudden I see the girl I love. I run to her and tell her that, although I am very poor, if I were king, I would marry her and make her my queen. When I sing this song, it's not a make-believe fairy tale at all, because in my mind it really happened!

Oh Dear, What Can the Matter Be?

This 200-year-old song from England is about a young woman longing for her loved one to come back from the county fair. She hopes that he'll bring her a small token that will show her that he misses her too. In this song, I'm singing of the sweetness of young love, so innocent and pure. Like many folk songs, however, later versions of this song were written with entirely different meanings. For instance, in 1864, a new version scolded parents for not visiting their children's schools. Another later version spoke out for the struggle to give women the right to vote. I think it's amazing to see how the interpretation of folk songs can change over the years.

Billy Boy

In the earliest known version of this song, which is based on an English ballad called "Lord Randall" from the 1700s, a mother questions her son about his loved one. This song is very sad, but the version of "Billy Boy" in this book, from a hundred years later, is all fun. Billy's mother only wants to know if her son's bride is suitable. Billy is so in love he can't think clearly enough to answer her seriously. In the wondrous way that folk music changes over the years, Bob Dylan took this theme and in the early 1960s, while staying in my home in Woodstock, New York, wrote a song that opens with the words "Where have you been, my blue-eyed son?" It's called "A Hard Rain's A-Gonna Fall," and it's about his vision of hard times ahead, with challenges for the world to overcome.

Ten Little Puppy Dogs

The original words of this famous 150-year-old American song, which was called "Ten Little Indians," seemed delightful when it was first written, but the song made fun of the children of the first Americans. To respect Native Americans, I did what many folk singers do with folk music. As with other songs in this book, I changed the words! (In folk music, that's okay, and part of the fun!) So, instead of singing "One little, two little, three little Indians," which was the original version, I count puppy dogs, chickens, and even porcupines. Now it's a really fun song and doesn't hurt anyone's feelings.

This Old Man

"This Old Man" is an example of how the early folk music of America was a melding of traditions from England with the music of African slaves in America. The words and the melody are from England, but it also has the spirit and rhythmic feel of the music that came to America through the spirituals sung by the slaves. When those two types of music came together, a new kind of music was born that became our own American music. That's how the blues started, as well as country music, jazz, and rock 'n' roll. Think about how amazing it is that the gift of the music of black people in America, combined with songs from England and other European countries, became the starting point of one of America's greatest gifts to itself, and to the world!

Polly Wolly Doodle

The first printed version of "Polly Wolly Doodle" appeared in a Harvard College student songbook from 1880. Children still love this song but it seems unlikely that college students of today would sing songs as silly as this one. Folk music can teach us much about how the world has changed. From this song, we can imagine how young college students around the turn of the last century may have felt at a party. When I imagine them singing this song, they seem much more innocent than college students today. See how folk music can lead you to all kinds of new thoughts and ideas?

Old MacDonald Had a Farm

Some songs start in one country and travel all over the world. That's the case with this song about Old MacDonald. It is thought that this song was first sung about 300 years ago as part of an opera called "The Kingdom of Birds." One song in the opera contained the lyrics "Booing here, booing there, here a boo, there a boo, everywhere a boo." Now, there are dozens of versions with different words translated into many different languages, such as Spanish, Portuguese, Mandarin, Arabic, Czech, Finnish, Hebrew, Japanese, and Farsi, just to name a few!

About the Author

Peter Yarrow's career has spanned close to five decades as a member of the legendary folk trio Peter, Paul & Mary, who became known to many as a voice of their generation's conscience, awakening and inspiring others to help make the world a more just, equitable, and peaceful place. Today, Yarrow devotes the majority of his time to running Operation Respect, a nonprofit he founded in 1999. Congress unanimously voted to honor Operation Respect's work creating respectful, safe, and bully-free environments for children in schools across America and beyond. Besides numerous awards for his artistry and his public service, Peter has received two honorary doctorates for his steadfast work in the educational arena.

For many years, Peter Yarrow dreamed of recording his favorite folk songs in a very simple, intimate way—the way he first heard them sung as a child. Along with his daughter, Bethany Yarrow, a gifted singer in her own right, Peter shares the songs that first moved and inspired him to become the renowned folk singer he is today. When asked what he would most want to give the generations that follow him, Peter said, "I would give them these songs that helped me come to realize what, for me, is really important in life—people, love, work, and service to each other. I believe that all children can be helped to discover what's important to them in their lives, through these songs. It's magic, in a way, but it seems to happen every time!"

About the Illustrator

Terry Widener's relationship with folk music began as a child in Oklahoma, where he was surrounded by classic folk songs performed by singers like Woody Guthrie. Folk music had made a big impact on the region during the Dustbowl era, and as Terry grew up, this music was an essential part of his heritage.

Inspired by a passion for art, Terry studied graphic design at the University of Tulsa. He has illustrated more than twenty books, including *If the Shoe Fits* by Gary Soto, *Steel Town* by Jonah Winter, and *Lou Gehrig: The Luckiest Man* by David Adler. His picture books have won numerous accolades including a Boston Globe–Horn Book Honor Award, an ALA Notable Children's Book Award, and the California Young Reader Medal.

A father of three, Terry currently resides in McKinney, Texas, with his wife, Leslie.

CD Credits

Produced by Peter Yarrow and Kevin Salem.

Peter Yarrow: Lead Vocals, Guitar.

Bethany Yarrow: Lead Vocals.

Mary Rower: Vocal Duet with Peter on "Oh Dear, What Can The Matter Be."

Paul Prestopino: Lead Guitar, Dobro, Ukulele, Banjo, Mandolin, Mandola, Harmonica.

John Conte: Bass.

Background Vocals: Delilah Dougan, Maralina Gabriel, Olivia Gabriel, Kasey Stelter, Mary Rower

Recorded, engineered, mixed and mastered by Kevin Salem, Woodstock, New York.

Special Thanks

Marcus Leaver, Frances Gilbert, Robert Agis, Leigh Ann Ambrosi, Paula Allen, Kaylee Davis, Derry Wilkens, Wendy Raffel, Rachel Jackson, Tony Arancio, Beth Bradford, Kate Hyman